Usborne
A Sticker Dolly Story
Woodland Princess

Zanna Davidson

Illustrated by Addy Rivera Sonda
Cover illustration by Antonia Miller

Use the stickers to dress the Dolls on the 'Meet the Dolls' pages

Meet the Princess Dolls

Meera, Sophia and Olivia are the 'Princess Dolls'. They help the princesses who live on the Majestic Isle, with everything from new outfits to royal emergencies.

Olivia

is a rebel princess. She spends as much time as she can outside. She loves plants and animals and is an excellent horse rider.

Use the stickers to dress the Dolls

Sophia
loves books and stories
about princesses of the past.
She is always calm in a crisis.
Her favourite place in the
world is the palace library.

Meera
is brilliant at making clothes
and jewellery. She is generous
and giving, and also likes
to follow royal rules.

Dolly Town

The Princess Dolls live in the Royal Palace, in Dolly Town,
home to all the Dolls. The Dolls work in teams to help those
in trouble and are the very best at what they do, whether
that's fashion design, ice skating or puppy training.
Each day brings with it an exciting new adventure…

The **Shooting Star** train
whisks the Dolls away
on their missions.

Madame Coco's
Costume Emporium
has everything the
Dolls might need.

The Dolls love to
celebrate at the
Cupcake Café.

Rose Theatre

Animal
Sanctuary

Bluebell Bookshop

Evergreen
Sports
Arena

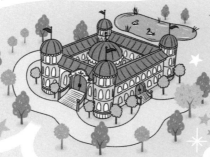

Royal Palace is home to the Princess Dolls.

Palm Tree Film Studios

HEARTBEAT

Heartbeat Dance Academy

Fashion Design Studio

Mission Control Centre lets the Dolls know who's in trouble and where to go.

Pop Star Stadium

SPARKLES

Silver Sparkles Skating Rink

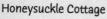

Honeysuckle Cottage

Strawberry Lane Stables

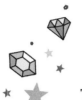

Chapter One
The Rebellious Princess

I t was a beautiful day in Dolly Town and the Princess Dolls were enjoying the spring sunshine in their palace conservatory.

"These flowers are so beautiful," said Meera, beginning to sketch them. "I'm going to use them in my next jewellery design."

"Don't forget we're going to the Cupcake Café later," said Olivia. "Maya has invited us to her Spring Celebration." She held out the invitation as she spoke.

Maya would like to invite
the **Princess Dolls**
to a **Spring
Celebration**
at her Cupcake Café.
There will be cake,
sparkling rose water,
music and spring flowers.

"How could I forget?" said
Meera. "Maya always makes the
best cakes!"

But just then all three of the Dolls' watches began to flash.

"It's Mission Control!" said Olivia, tapping the flashing tiara symbol on her watch. "Come in, Mission Control. It's Olivia here."

"We have a new mission for you," said Mission Control. "Are all the Princess Dolls there?"

"Yes we're all here," said Olivia. "What's happened?"

"There's a princess in trouble on the Majestic Isle," said Mission Control.

"Oh no! Which princess?" asked Sophia.

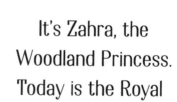

It's Zahra, the Woodland Princess. Today is the Royal Family Portrait. The most famous artist on the Majestic Isle is coming to the Woodland Kingdom to paint them, but the Woodland Princess has run away!

"But why?" asked Meera.

"She was given an outfit especially for the occasion, but she hated it! She ran off into the woods and tore her dress climbing a tree, and now she's in a panic. She never meant to ruin her outfit. Zahra's still hiding in the woods as she doesn't want her parents to see, but she really needs a new dress and fast. Can you help?"

"Of course we can," said Olivia.

"Mission details coming through now," said Mission Control.

Sophia ran over to a side table and picked up her gold-cased screen, just as the mission details flashed up.

We haven't been to the Woodland Kingdom before.

MISSION INFORMATION:

Mission to the Woodland Kingdom

Zahra facts:

Likes:

Climbing trees and running.
Being rebellious and athletic.
Spending time outdoors.

Needs:

A dress for the Royal Portrait,
which starts today at 3pm,
outside the Treetop Palace.

ZAHRA THE WOODLAND PRINCESS

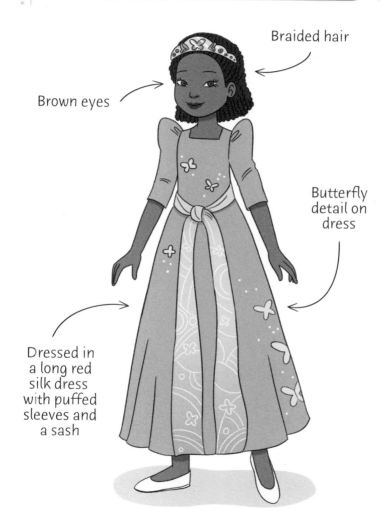

Braided hair

Brown eyes

Butterfly detail on dress

Dressed in a long red silk dress with puffed sleeves and a sash

MISSION LOCATION:

Woodland Kingdom

Border of **River Kingdom**

Butterfly Fields

Acacia
Avenue

Honey
Grove

Shining Stream

Palace
Gardens

X
Wildflower
Glade

*Woodland Princess
last seen here*

"I've been longing to visit the Woodland Kingdom," said Olivia. "It'll be so beautiful now, just after the first rains. And best of all, it's home to the rarest bird on the Majestic Isle – the jewel bird. It would be amazing if we saw one."

"It seems like one of our more straightforward missions, too," added Sophia with a smile. "We should be back in time for the Spring Celebration." She spoke into her watch. "Mission Control – we'll be there as soon as we can."

Meera turned to the others.
"First we'll need mission outfits,"
she said. "And of course a new
dress for Zahra."

"Well we all know the best place
to go…" said Olivia.

"Madame Coco's Costume
Emporium!" they all chanted
together.

Chapter Two

Mission Outfits

The Princess Dolls picked up their bags, put on their sunglasses, and stepped out of the palace.

Outside, the sun shone, there was a warm breeze and the air was filled with the sweet scent of spring flowers.

It wasn't long before the Princess Dolls were standing outside Madame Coco's, gazing up at the window displays and the flags, fluttering in the breeze.

They made their way through the revolving door, past counters selling everything from perfume to parasols, and over to the famous glass elevator.

"Good morning, Princess Dolls," said Jasper, the lift attendant, standing smartly to attention in his gold and blue uniform. "Where would you like to go today?"

"The Royal Department floor, please Jasper," said Sophia.

"Right away," said Jasper, smiling at them from under his peaked cap.

He pressed
the button and
the glass elevator
glided up and up
before coming
to a stop with
a gentle

TING!

The doors
opened to reveal
a vast room
sparkling with
jewels.

Chandeliers hung from the ceiling. There were beautiful dresses at every turn, and low tables overflowing with necklaces and tiaras. And gliding towards them, looking as glamorous as ever, was Madame Coco herself.

"Good day, Princess Dolls," she said, in her soft French accent. "Are you here on a new mission?"

"Yes," said Sophia, excitedly. "We're going to the Woodland Kingdom on the Majestic Isle. Zahra, the Woodland Princess, urgently needs a new dress to wear for the Royal Family Portrait."

"I see," said Madame Coco. "Did you have anything in mind?"

"Here's a picture of her last outfit," said Sophia, holding out the picture on her screen.

"It's beautiful, but Zahra really didn't like it. Maybe she was put off by the rich colour? Or the length?"

"We know she loves climbing trees and being outdoors," said Meera, "so I was wondering if we could find her a green dress, and one that's easy to move in. Perhaps it could be the colour of forest leaves, with jewels to match – emeralds, or malachite, or jade?"

As she spoke, she swiped her screen to show Madame Coco the picture of Zahra that Mission Control had sent them.

"I've read that the butterfly is the symbol of the Woodland Kingdom," added Sophia. "It would be lovely if we could work that into the outfit in some way."

"I have just the thing," said Madame Coco. "Wait there!"

She returned moments later with a beautiful green and gold dress. "I call this our Forest Rain Dress," said Madame Coco. "It makes me think of

the flush of new leaves that mark the start of the rainy season."

"Oh, it's perfect!" said Meera, leaning in for a closer look. "I love the gold sash, and the butterfly detail on the sleeves."

"It seems to sparkle, too," added Olivia.

"There's an overlay of glitter," said Madame Coco. "And there's this to go with it…" she added, opening a silk jewel case to reveal a delicate gold leaf tiara, studded with emeralds.

Zahra's clothes

Shoes with butterfly detail

Gold leaf tiara, encrusted with emeralds

'Forest Rain Dress' with gold sash

"Lucky Zahra," said Meera, beaming at her. "Thank you, Madame Coco."

"And don't think I've forgotten about you three," added Madame Coco, with a twinkle in her eye. "You'll be needing your mission outfits. Something regal, yet just right for trekking through woods."

As she spoke, she clicked her fingers and her assistants hurried over, their arms laden with clothes.

Olivia's clothes

Green
jumpsuit with
a scoop neck

Brown boots
with gold laces

Sophia's clothes

Flowing blue dress with crossover ribbons

Soft brown boots

Meera's clothes

Gold silk belt

Purple lace-up boots with cross stitching

Knee-length tunic dress with star embroidery

Then, as the Princess Dolls' names flashed up above the changing rooms, they stepped inside...

When they stepped out again,
they were dressed and ready for
their mission.

"And here are three cloaks," said Madame Coco, "to keep you warm in the shady woods. And last but not least…" she handed over Zahra's outfit, in a boutique bag.

"Thank you!" said the Dolls.

Then they
whooshed back
down in the lift
and hurried
outside, onto
the sunny street
once more.

"That's odd," said Sophia, looking
down at her wrist. "Our watches
have started flashing. I wonder why
Mission Control is calling us again..."

"Come in," she said, tapping
the tiara symbol on her watch.
"What's happened?"

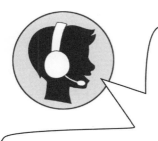

It's the Woodland Princess. She asked for help, but now we can't contact her. She was last seen in the Wildflower Glade. Please be as quick as you can, Princess Dolls. We don't know what's happened to her!

Chapter Three

Into the Woods

"We must hurry," said Sophia, tapping her watch again, this time to summon the Shooting Star train. Moments later, it appeared before them, in a glittering cloud of dust.

"Where would you like
to go today, Princess Dolls?"
asked Sienna, the train driver.

"The Wildflower Glade on the
Majestic Isle, please," said Olivia.
"As fast as you can."

"Climb aboard!" said Sienna.

The Princess Dolls stepped inside the train. The doors glided shut and then they were off, speeding through Dolly Town.

Before long, they entered a dark tunnel, sparkling with hundreds of tiny stars.

With a

WHOOSH

the train shot out the other side.

"Look!" cried Meera. "We're on the Majestic Isle. This must be the Woodland Kingdom."

The train was now whizzing along a narrow path. On either side were beautiful trees, their trunks gleaming golden-brown and silvery-white.

The Shooting Star slowed, then came to a smooth stop in a clearing.

"Here we are, Princess Dolls," said Sienna. "Good luck with your mission."

"Thank you," said the Dolls, as they stepped off the train.

They all turned to wave as Sienna sped away in another glittering cloud of dust.

For a moment, the Princess Dolls stood in the clearing, looking around for the Woodland Princess. Sunbirds flitted from flower to flower, parrots squawked from the

treetops and a warm breeze wafted over them. But there was no sign of Zahra.

"We're in the right place," said Sophia, checking the map. "I can see the turrets of the Treetop Palace, and a glint of the Shining Stream between those trees, so this must be it."

"We'd better call for her," said Meera. She cupped her hands around her mouth and began to call out.

Zahra! *Zah-ra!*

There was no answer. The only sound was the babbling stream, the calling birds and the rustle of leaves in the wind.

"Look!" said Olivia, suddenly. She pointed to a tangle of brambles, and there, among the thorns, was a strip of red silk, fluttering in the breeze. "This is from Zahra's dress. She must have come this way…"

Then a creaking noise above made them all glance up.

"Oh!" said Sophia. "Did you see that? Up there! A flash of red in the leaves."

The Princess Dolls walked over to the nearest tree. Just visible in the branches, high above, was a girl.

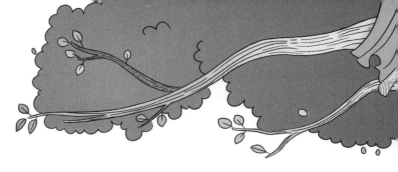

Her dress was torn and dirty,
her face was smudged with tears
and her hair was full of twigs.

"Zahra!" called Olivia. "Is
that you?"

"Yes!" Zahra replied, realizing
she'd been seen. "It is me but I've
changed my mind. I don't need your
help after all. I'm *not* going to the
Royal Portrait and there's nothing
you can say that will make me!"

Chapter Four

The
Treetop Palace

Sophia turned to the other Dolls. "What do we do now?" she said in a low whisper. "How are we going to persuade Zahra to come down?"

But Olivia had already started taking off her cloak and bag. "I think it's time to use my tree climbing skills," she said with a smile.

"I can't design beautiful clothes
and jewellery like you, Meera.
And I don't have Sophia's
knowledge from books,
but I can climb trees!"
On those words, she
swung herself up
from a low-
hanging branch.

Meera and Sophia watched
as she clambered from branch to
branch, moving swiftly and quietly.

"She's like a ballet dancer
among the branches!" said Sophia,
admiringly.

It wasn't long before Olivia was
nearing Zahra's branch, but Zahra
was already on the move, reaching
for the branches above.

"Zahra, wait!" said Olivia. "I've come to talk to you, nothing else. We've brought you a dress to wear for the Royal Portrait, just as you asked, but if you decide you really don't want to go, I won't make you."

"Really?" said Zahra, turning back.

"I promise," said Olivia. "Just tell me what happened."

Zahra looked at her, as if to make sure Olivia was telling the truth, then climbed back down the branch to sit beside Olivia.

"I didn't expect you to be able to reach me," Zahra admitted. "My parents are always telling me that princesses shouldn't climb trees."

"Well this one does," said Olivia, smiling at her. "Now, tell me, what's going on?"

Zahra took a deep breath. "It's all because of the Royal Portrait," she began. "My brothers and my sister

were so excited, getting dressed up
and putting on their best clothes.
My parents made me put on this
dress…but I made a big fuss as I
hate it. It's so long I can hardly
move in it without tripping up, and

it's so heavy I can't *do* anything…"
She paused for a moment, fiddling
with the frayed hem of her dress.

"Go on," said Olivia gently.

"Well, I did put on the dress
eventually, but my
parents told me
not to go
outside, so I
wouldn't get
dirty. But I
knew I'd never
be able to keep
still for the

portrait if I didn't just have a quick run outside. But when I reached the glade, I realized I'd torn my dress  on the spiky thorns and I knew my parents would be furious *and* think I'd done it on purpose, so that's when I asked for help. But as I waited for you to come, I just got angrier and angrier!"

"Why was that?" asked Olivia.

"I don't think I should even *be* in the Royal Portrait," said Zahra, miserably. "I don't like wearing dresses and jewels. All I really like doing is climbing trees, and my parents don't approve of that." She paused for a moment to wipe her face on her muddy sleeve. "I just don't think I make a very good princess…"

"All princesses are different," said Olivia, "and that's a good thing. It would be very boring if we were all the same. Look at us," she went on, gesturing down to the other Princess Dolls. "I like caring for animals and being outdoors, Sophia likes reading, and Meera loves clothes and jewels. That doesn't make any one of us a better princess than the other, does it?"

"No, I suppose not," said Zahra, doubtfully.

"The important thing is that we all want to help people," Olivia went on. "You see *that's* what makes a good princess."

"Really?" asked Zahra.

"Definitely," said Olivia. "*And*
doing the right thing…"

Zahra looked up at Olivia. "I
suppose that includes being there
for the Royal Portrait?"

Olivia nodded. "Imagine how
unhappy your parents would be if
you weren't in the portrait. And

then afterwards, you can reward yourself with some tree climbing."

Zahra shook her head. "My parents won't let me do that," she said, "but I can see that you're right. I can't miss the Royal Portrait. It would make my parents really sad…" She gave a sigh. "I suppose I'd better go back to the palace and get ready. Will you come too?" she added, shyly. "It might not feel so bad if you're there."

"Of course I'll be there," said Olivia, smiling at her.

Back on the ground, Zahra led
the Princess Dolls towards the
Treetop Palace.

"We couldn't help overhearing
your conversation," Meera whispered
to Olivia as they walked. "I've been
trying to think of a way to cheer
Zahra up. It would be wonderful if
we could do something for her…"

But she stopped speaking as the
Treetop Palace rose into view,
gleaming silver-white among the trees.

"Oh, wow!" exclaimed Sophia.
"I've seen pictures of the palace in
my book…"

I hadn't expected it
to be this beautiful.

The palace was nestled in a ring of trees, its walls carved from silvery wood.

"These trees are called butterfly trees," explained Zahra, "as butterflies flock here once a year, covering the branches. Each part of the palace is connected by treetop walkways."

"How do you get inside?"
asked Meera.

"That's almost the best part!"
said Zahra, her eyes lighting up
for a moment.

She led them inside a hollow

tree, where a staircase
wound its way up the
tree's trunk, right into
the heart of the palace.

They came out into a room that
encircled the trunk of the great
butterfly tree. From here, the Dolls
could see corridors stretching away
in all directions.

"I'll just go to my room and get changed," said Zahra. "I won't be long. You can wait here," she went on, gesturing to some gleaming gold chairs, clustered around a little table.

When Zahra returned, she was wearing the dress from Madame Coco's, along with the beautiful tiara. Behind her, came the King and Queen.

"Thank you for the dress," said Zahra. "It's so comfortable. It's lovely to be able to move freely."

"You look wonderful," said Meera.

The Queen stepped forward to greet them. "Zahra has told us how you came to help today. Thank you – all of you."

Then she turned to her daughter. "Zahra," she said, nodding towards the staircase, "you go ahead with your father. I'll be down in a moment."

Once they'd gone, the Queen carried on in a low voice. "Zahra has never liked dressing up, or attending functions. She's always been a bit of a rebel. We hoped she would grow out of it, but she doesn't seem to be…"

"I've been trying to think of something that might cheer Zahra up," said Meera. "And I think I've

come up with a good idea, but I
wanted to make sure you approved."

She leant over and whispered to
the Queen.

The Queen smiled and whispered
back. Then Meera beckoned to
Sophia. "Come with me," she said.
"I have an idea and I'm going to
need your help…"

Chapter Five

Princesses
to the Rescue

Outside in the palace gardens, Olivia watched as the artist arranged the royal family for the portrait. She could see Zahra was trying her hardest to be good.

"I need you to stay as still as you can," said the artist, lifting up her paintbrush.

But as she spoke, there was a commotion in the branches above them. Everyone looked up.

"What is it?" said the King. "Something's squawking."

"It sounds like a jewel bird," said the Queen. She turned to the Dolls. "They're extremely rare and are only found here, in our Woodland Kingdom."

"I've read all about them," said Olivia, excitedly, hurrying over to the tree.

"It *is* a jewel bird!" said Zahra, pointing up into the branches. "Up there! I can see its glittering feathers."

"Oh no!" she added suddenly.
"The jewel birds are squawking
because the palace cat is up there.
He's heading straight for their nest!"

They all watched as the parent
birds flew around the cat. But the

cat kept creeping along the
branch, getting nearer and nearer
to the nest. Then, at the last
moment, the baby bird jumped
from the nest and tumbled onto
the branch below.

"The baby's flapping about," said
Zahra. "It's going to fall! And the
cat looks like it's going to pounce..."

"Oh poor little thing," said
the Queen.

As she spoke, the baby bird
tried to fly again, but its little
wings weren't ready.

Zahra tried to shout up to the cat, to shoo it away, but it stayed where it was, its eyes fixed on the baby bird.

"I know the portrait's important," said Zahra, "but we have to try and save the baby jewel bird. There are so few of them left. It's so important that every chick survives."

"You can't," insisted the King. "It's far too high. And too dangerous. And besides," he added, "you know what I think about princesses climbing trees!"

Olivia stepped forward. "I'll go with her," she said. "I've read about the jewel bird. I'll do anything to help. I couldn't bear just to sit here and do nothing."

Please...?

The King and Queen exchanged glances. The artist shrugged. "I can wait!" she said. "If you're all worrying about this baby bird, then none of you will be looking your best for my portrait!"

The Queen turned to Zahra. "Are you sure you can do this?" she asked.

Zahra nodded.

"Then go," said the Queen. "There's no time for you to change, but do try not to ruin another dress! And please – be careful."

Together, Zahra and Olivia began to climb the tree.

"I'm just behind you if you fall," said Olivia, as they edged higher and higher. Looking down, Olivia could see the ground, far below them. It was as if they were in their own little world among the rustling leaves.

As soon as the cat saw them coming, it bolted down the tree. But the baby jewel bird was still flapping around on the branch, and Zahra could see that its legs

had become tangled in the vine
around the tree. It was never going
to get out on its own.

"Don't worry," Zahra whispered.
"We're here to help."

"You're smaller than me," said
Olivia, "so it makes more sense
for you to edge along the branch.

See if you can free the jewel bird,
then pass it back to me, and I'll
put the baby bird back in its nest."

Zahra nodded. She laid herself
flat along the branch and crept
forwards, all the while talking in
a low voice, trying to keep the
bird calm.

At last, she was close enough to touch the vines around the jewel bird's feet. She carefully untangled them, then gently scooped up the baby jewel bird in her hands.

"Oh he's so tiny," she whispered to Olivia. "And so fluffy! Only now...I don't know how I'm going

to get back to you and hold him at the same time."

She looked at Olivia, and then down at the ground so far below and began to wobble. "Oh no," she said, panic in her eyes. "I'm not sure I can do this! I think I'm stuck…"

Chapter Six
A Royal Outfit

Olivia locked eyes with Zahra. "Just stay exactly as you are," she said, "and take a deep breath. I'll reach across and get the jewel bird from you."

"Are you sure?" said Zahra.

Olivia nodded. "Don't worry," she said. "We can do this."

Olivia wrapped one arm around the trunk of the tree and reached out with her other, as far as she could go. "Now you just need to turn slightly," she said. "And pass him to me. Don't look down. Keep your eyes fixed on me."

Zahra took a deep breath. She grasped the branch with her legs and turned towards Olivia, then gave a gasp as the branch shook with her movement.

"Well done," said Olivia, in a steady voice. "That's perfect.

Just lean a little closer…That's it!"

With outstretched fingers, Olivia slid her hand beneath Zahra's, cupping the baby jewel bird in her palm.

Then, slowly and carefully, she drew away again.

"Well done, Zahra," Olivia said, beaming at her. "Now inch backwards along the branch. You've done it before. You can do it again."

"I'm okay now," said Zahra, with a faint smile. "I can do this."

"I just need to put this little baby back," said Olivia. "Wait there, and then I'll climb down the tree with you."

A moment later, Olivia was shimmying up the trunk of the tree, until she reached the nest. Then she gently placed the baby bird inside.

Above her, the parent jewel birds squawked and fluttered. "I hope they go back to their baby, and that we haven't scared them away," she thought.

Then Olivia
swung down
again, until she
was below Zahra,
and they both
came down the
tree together.

When they reached the ground they looked up, and gave a little cheer.

"Look!" said Zahra. "The jewel bird's parents have returned to the nest. We did it! We really did it!"

"Well done," said the King, beaming at Zahra. "I had no idea you could climb like that. I'm so proud of you. And you rescued a jewel bird."

But then Zahra looked down at her dress. "I'm sorry," she said, ruefully. "I'm covered in dirt again. I really am a hopeless princess…"

"Is that what you think?" asked the King.

Zahra nodded.

"Well it's not true," said the Queen. "You're a wonderful princess. Look how brave you've just been."

"But I don't do proper princess things," said Zahra, looking at her parents. "I'm always getting in trouble for climbing trees and ruining my dresses…"

Before they could reply, they saw
Meera and Sophia, coming towards
them across the palace lawn.

"Is this a good time?" asked Meera.

"It's perfect," said the Queen.

"In that case," said Sophia,
turning to Zahra, "we've got
something for you…"

I think you're
going to love it!

And she held out a beautiful outfit patterned in blue, gold and green.

"Meera designed it, and I helped her make it," said Sophia. "It's a 'Princess Tree Climbing Outfit'. We've made it out of a stretchy fabric, so you can climb easily, and even though it looks silky, it's tough too, so it won't snag and tear."

"And the fabric is waterproof," said Meera, "so you can go out in all weathers."

"And look," added Sophia, "it has pockets too, for you to put things in. Perfect for treetop adventures!"

"Oh!" gasped Zahra. "It's amazing. I love it!"

"Well," said the Queen. "You had better go and put it on."

"Really?" asked Zahra. "But what about the Royal Portrait?"

"We want you to wear it *for* the portrait," said the Queen.

The King nodded. "We hated that you felt you had to run away from the portrait. And you were so brave, saving that baby jewel bird. I think it's time we let you be who you are," he said. "A tree climbing princess! I can't think of anything better for you to wear in our family portrait."

"I'll run and put it on now," said Zahra, grinning.

Then she turned to the Princess Dolls. "Thank you!" she said. "For all your help today."

"It was our pleasure," said Olivia.

When Zahra came back, her head was held high. "I feel like I could climb a thousand trees in this," she said, proudly. "But I promise I'll keep perfectly still for the portrait," she added, smiling at the artist.

After everyone had said goodbye,
the Princess Dolls headed back
towards the palace. Sophia tapped
the tiara symbol on her watch, and
moments later, Sienna drew up
in a glittering cloud of dust.

"We'd like to go to the Cupcake Café to celebrate, please," said Olivia, smiling at her. But before they could step aboard, they heard a shout, and one of the royal servants came hurrying out to them.

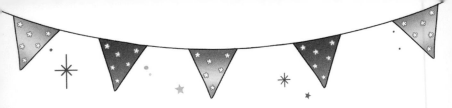

"Princess Zahra wanted you to have these," he said, handing them three beautifully wrapped gifts. "They're to say thank you for all you did today. She'd like you to open them when you get home…"

Back at the Cupcake Café, the Princess Dolls were just in time

for the Spring Celebration.
They settled down in their
favourite seats by the window.
Before them, plates were piled
high with delicious cakes and the
whole café had been decked out
with beautiful spring flowers.

After greeting all their friends,
they waited until there was a
quiet moment. "Shall we open

our presents now?" said Meera.

"Let's!" agreed Sophia.

"On the count of three," said Meera.

They unravelled the ribbons and wrapping paper and let out a gasp.

"Oh!" said Sophia. "A book all about the Woodland Kingdom."

"And I've been given a beautiful butterfly necklace," said Meera. "What have you got, Olivia?"

Olivia beamed.

"A tiny little jewel bird, carved from wood," she said. "There's a note from Zahra, saying it's from her own collection. She wanted me to have it, as something to remember her by. Isn't that lovely!"

"Another successful mission," said Sophia, smiling back at her. "I can't wait for our next one."

Then the three Princess Dolls

put out their hands and laid them one on top of each other. "Princess Dolls forever!" they chanted.

The End

Join the **Princess Dolls** on their next adventure in

Usborne
A Sticker Dolly Story
Waterlily Ball

with stickers

Zanna Davidson

Read on for a sneak peek...

"We've got a new mission!" said Sophia, excitedly.

"Let's find out what it is!" said Meera, tapping her screen.

"Are you all there?" asked Mission Control.

"Yes," replied Meera, as Olivia and Sophia gathered round the

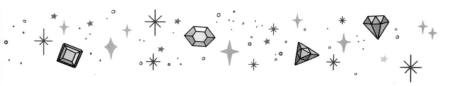

gold-cased screen. "All three Princess Dolls are here. And we're mission-ready!"

"Is there a problem on the Majestic Isle?" asked Sophia.

"I'm afraid so," replied Mission Control. "This time it's in the River Kingdom, in the west.

The River Princess is in desperate need of your help.

Tonight is the Waterlily Ball, to celebrate the end of the rainy season, but the River Princess says something terrible has happened. She wouldn't tell us any more than that. Will you accept the mission?"

The Dolls all nodded.

"We'll come as soon as we can," promised Olivia. Then she turned to the others. "We'd better get our mission outfits," she said.

"First stop, Madame Coco's Costume Emporium," they chanted together.

Edited by Lesley Sims and Stephanie King
Designed by Hannah Cobley and Hope Reynolds

First published in 2021 by Usborne Publishing Ltd.,
Usborne House, 83-85 Saffron Hill, London EC1N 8RT, England.
usborne.com Copyright © 2021 Usborne Publishing Ltd. UKE